AF603738

THE AUTHOR

Biljana Veljkovic

ISBN-978-86-906998-2-7

ADVENTURE, FANTASY

Summary of the Act

PRINCESS

Iva of Serbia

While she carelessly saw her childhood, things changed in an instant, Serbia was mowed down by a wave of Turks and changed her life forever. Her brother was taken by the Janissaries, her parents were executed. Saved from the Turks, she grew up with a great desire for revenge, which will turn little Iva into the greatest warrior in Serbia. In this she will be helped by the old servant Milivoje and many other brave people who will protect her at the cost of their lives. In that campaign, Philip will join her with a group of subjects. Princess Iva and Philip will become closer even though danger lurks from every angle, as they prepare for the biggest battle.

Biljana Veljkovic

Princess Iva of Serbia

The story was told by Milivoje's
old servant as he remembered it...

* * *

Once upon a time, in the distant past, there was a beautiful kingdom that is now forgotten - a kingdom of warriors and proud people. Serbs inhabited these areas for centuries, long before my memory began. Most people considered them honest, brave, prudent and hardworking people. They are one of the oldest nations in this region, which never surrendered to enemy forces.

Serbs were known as a nation that resisted the challenges of time and enemies. Their ferocity and steadfastness were known throughout the world. Although time has brought changes, and the number of people may have decreased, the Serbian spirit has remained unquenchable, carrying with it the pride and strength that were the inheritance of generations.

The Serbs were truly outstanding horsemen and warriors, often described as tall and strong men, with broad shoulders and strong arms. This physical strength probably stems from the fact that Serbia was built on very fertile soil, where people were taught from a young age to work hard and help with various jobs, such as building houses, boats and other construction projects.

Many Serbs were engaged in agriculture, animal husbandry, blacksmithing, construction and fishing. Surrounded by numerous mountains and mines, the Serbs had a wealth of natural resources at their disposal. However, what gave them the most pleasure was living near water.

They are known for their cheerful spirit and hospitality. For Serbs, it is a great honor to host someone in their home, and they will gladly offer their guests food, drinks and good entertainment with music. Their selflessness is reflected in their willingness to share everything they have with others, even the last slice of cake.

Over the imposing mountain peaks that rise to the very clouds, down winding streams and rivers rich in fish, you reach the heart of the kingdom of the Serbs. An ancient people who have been living in peace and harmony for centuries, defending their land against all challenges. In that kingdom, King Stefan ruled together with his beloved wife Jelena.

King Stephen was an imposing man of tall stature, with broad shoulders and a prominent mustache that swayed in the wind as he rode his favorite one horse. His sharp, green eyes shone from under thick brows, carefully surveying every man who came near him.

Revered for his righteousness and devotion to protecting his people, King Stefan was a symbol of courage and leadership. He spent more time among his soldiers on the battlefield than in the comfort of his castle. Although brave and warlike, he was modest and durable, moving easily and reacting quickly, often surprising his opponents with his skill and unexpected moves.

As a skilled military leader, his mere presence on the battlefield was enough to cause confusion among the enemy ranks. He shared the hardships of camp and field life with his soldiers, truly inspiring them with his example. In battle, he was always the leader of his troops, encouraging them to go forward, fearlessly defending his country.
Queen Jelena was a quiet and gentle woman, endowed with a distinct beauty that came from her long blonde locks that fell over her shoulders. Caring and warm, she devotedly cared for all the subjects of her kingdom. She often visited bazaars, embroidered and spent time in the garden behind the castle, arranging it with love and care. She shared her love and devotion to her country with King Stefan, and their son Mihailo was their greatest joy.

Mihajlo was a lively and sweet child, who loved to sneak into the kitchen more than anything. While the old cooks were preparing the feast, he would sneak under the table, stealing a treat. Their family came from old and proud kings, whose ancestors defended and protected their land from enemies for centuries.

One unforgettable day, a little princess-za Ivo was born in the royal home, bringing with her joy and happiness to the hearts of her parents and the entire kingdom.

I remember that it was the month of the sun and that summer had begun... you could say it was the month of June. The news quickly spread throughout the kingdom. All the halls were busy preparing for the festivities and making a feast, as befits a princess.

The maids set the tables with the silver escaik, they ironed it until it shone so that it sparkled before the eyes. White tablecloths were placed with decorated lace falling over the edges of the table. This room was decorated with special care. The interior was decorated with tories and expensive fabrics. The cooks prepared various dishes day and night, deliciously prepared game, boar and deer, but also birds such as pheasants, quails and partridges. Wine and beer were drunk. Fish from the surrounding lake was also eaten. The water in the lake was so clear, blue and huge that it resembled the sea. On the mountain at the southern end, there was a spring of water that poured out and descended over a high waterfall. In the summer, in the quiet evening hours, the noise of the waterfall could be heard through the air like a distant rumble.

Treats were prepared from various types of fruit (of which Serbia never lacked) and honey. Cabbage salads, green salad, radishes sprinkled with honey were a real treat. The sauces were made from various types of mushrooms such as porcini mushrooms and morels, freshly picked in the nearby forests.

The castle itself, located on a high rise, offered a wonderful view of the town below. It was decorated with welcome flags, made of light silk fabric in red and blue tones, with the symbol of a double-headed eagle looking in both directions, its wings raised high as if ready to fly immediately. This symbol represented the unity of the kingdom, the readiness to defend and the pride of the Serbs.

In the immediate vicinity of the castle, there was a small church that has withstood the test of time for years. It was situated at the foot of a great mountain by the shore of a lake, which was so wide that the opposite shores seemed small and distant. It was so long that its northern end, which looked towards the mountain, could not be seen. with special attention paid to the symmetrical layout of the rooms. Twenty spacious and luxurious rooms provided comfort and elegance, while the large summer balcony with its view of the garden, full of wonderful greenery and flowers, was a favorite place to relax and enjoy. This castle was richly decorated with wrought iron and copper ornaments, with lavishly decorated columns and balconies that stretched towards the western part of the castle, offering an incredible view of the sunset. Walks through the garden were a delight, while the paths led past pine trees and large fir trees, adding magic to every step. At the entrance to the castle stood a mighty gate, whose heavy wooden doors were guarded by guards, trained and equipped for every possible situation. This castle was a symbol of strength and security, but also of luxurious style and elegance, which reflected the dignity and greatness of the kingdom of the Serbs.

The stables with the horses were getting ready to welcome the new arrivals, the horses were groomed and beautified, King Stefan himself was proud of his stable, which had hundreds of horses, from the most beautiful stallions to tame and strong mares.

King Stephen ordered to set aside the most beautiful pony for the princess. They chose a beautiful white horse with a wonderful mane, which the chief groom spent days grooming and preparing to be worthy of a princess. He was simply beautiful, so white that it was hard to look at him as the sun shone on his body. He had a long head, a noble and benevolent profile. His ears were small while his eyes were huge and prominent. White as snow and yet so bright that it almost sparkled in the moonlight, just like the stars in the sky. The celebration lasted 3 days and 3 nights. All the people from the town were invited to the feast, followed by a ceremony with the presence of the hall and other distinguished persons, and whoever was not near, King Stefan sent to every village, every town in the kingdom, food and drink (various fruits and vegetables with salted meat and with the wheat they used to wash the cake) which they distributed to the people in honor of the princess's birth. Because of his generosity, the people of Serbia greatly appreciated and loved their king, who always took care of his subjects.

Everyone from the surrounding towns gathered to pay their respects to King Stefan and bring gifts for the little princess. Subjects arrived with various presents and gifts that Serbia had never seen before. They were golden rattles, wooden horses hand-made and decorated with the finest threads, fabrics from distant lands woven in golden threads and decorated with pearls.

The local women made costumes for the little princess with love and devotion day and night, every stitch of the needle was full of tenderness and attention, and the fabrics were woven with red, gold and blue threads, decorated with floral motifs and symbols of the country.

Gifts included necklaces, ducats, pearls, mirrors with gold frames, and tiaras, which were a symbol of royal dignity and beauty. Each gift was an expression of respect and love for the royal family, and the presence of the subjects and their generosity added a special glow to the festivities and joy that filled the castle.

Prince Mihailo watched everything with excitement but also with a little jealousy, until he himself decided to visit his sister. He passed through a huge corridor decorated with paintings by old masters, various natures and places he hoped to visit someday when he was old enough.

He easily crossed the large blue carpet with its embroidery decorated and complemented the corridor, to the small room, the door of which was ajar. Inside was a cradle and the light was dimmed by large curtains that descended from the ceiling to the floor. He slowly approached the cradle. The cradle was carved with waves surrounding it, decorated with leaves and flowers and above it stretched a large white canopy made of pure white lace that covered part of the cradle. While at the bottom there were separate rocker-faces. Mihailo stood up on his toes and peered in to see the strange creature that had been talked about so much. He leaned his head straight into the cradle and saw his little sister. She had slightly golden hair and playful eyes covered by thick eyelashes. He immediately liked her and fell in love almost at the same moment.

He caressed her hair and discovered how sweet and dear she is, just like a little gem that needs to be faithfully looked after and protected. He promised her then, that he would take care of her and love her forever. As the princess grew, everyone in the court loved her very much. She was a happy and cheerful child. Prince Mihailo had a lot of fun with her. They played whenever they had the chance, because he, as the future heir, had a lot of responsibilities - for which an eight-year old can have. The youngest members of the royal family started training as soon as they were old enough to sit at the table. Children were brought up with formal lunches and events.

Formality was an essential part of the young prince's life, both in the way he spoke and in his clothing. His education included a variety of activities, such as riding lessons, learning to read, write and speak at least two other languages. He also had a mathematics teacher who came all the way from Vienna to teach him, although he found the

subject boring, the prince made efforts to please his father.
Political education was also mandatory, which entailed learning maps, maps and borders of states, as well as knowing their leaders.
Riding stood out as the most important skill that the young prince had to master, because it was not only a symbol of royal power but also a key skill for leading the army and maintaining order in the kingdom.

His earliest memories were of being mounted on a horse, it was amazing how regularly he fell off the broad, slippery backs of those huge, tall animals. He cried, but he was not afraid to succeed again when a horse was brought to him. The king's horseman Srdan was in charge of learning. He was a man who loved horses more than people. He spoke gently to the animals, so that even the most fearful ones stood obediently under the soothing hand he used to caress them. He had a young apprentice who took care of the animals themselves with the others. He didn't just shoe the horses, he also took care of their legs and hooves.

Later came more serious riding lessons with a great knight who was not only a magnificent warrior, but also a man of the king's greatest trust.
He was a member of the Knights of the Dragon. Chivalry was deeply rooted in Serbia as part of a rich warrior tradition, and Serbian knights were considered top warriors with the most lethal equipment. Warriors for whom faith, family and the Motherland were sacred.

In order to become and be a knight, a period of more than a decade was needed. As little boys of seven years old, they start learning, while at the age of 14 they become "shield bearers" with more serious training. They are introduced to weapons, taught to hunt and ride horses, and then after the age of twenty they acquire the right to prove themselves and become knights. He was majestic looking with dark hair, bushy eyebrows and a slightly darker complexion. Whenever Mihailo saw him in black shiny armor that covered his entire body, galloping towards the young prince on a horse with a light helmet, he admired him and secretly watched him, wishing that one day he too would look like that. As he was already middle-aged and peace had followed Serbia for some time, the knight spent his time going to tournaments, just to show the younger ones that he was still the strongest. From victory to victory, building strength and maintaining skill.

It wasn't long before Princess Iva was ready to study. Like her brother, she was taught by Srdan, but unlike Mihajlo, she was very gifted. Without any effort, riding lessons came naturally to her. It was as if she had always been on a horse. Soon she overcame even the most difficult obstacles effortlessly. She would sneak up to the barn whenever she had the chance and pet her pet. She and her white horse became an overnight sensation. Everyone came to watch her parade on a white horse. She was sitting straight on her horse, holding her bridle properly, her heels firmly down in the stirrups, the horse's mane flying and swaying with hers in rhythm. Everyone at court was very proud of her. She enjoyed riding, on that beautiful estate, surrounded by hundreds of years of history and the great blue sky above her.

* * *

As she grew up, she had less and less time to play with her brother Mihajlo, so they sneaked out in the summer and went to the shore of the lake to swim. Only the old servant followed them in the shadows and watched over them. One day they agreed to meet after class and swim because the day was getting hotter. Under the strong sun, in the middle of summer, the children jumped from shade to shade, so as not to burn their feet on the hot stones around the lake. Iva was already on the shore and was waiting for her brother, shuffling her feet, when she heard the cannons.

She was very scared and jumped to her feet. She wanted to run home but the old servant jumped out and put his hand over her mouth and silenced her, so that she wouldn't accidentally speak and give away their position.

The Turks, thirsty for conquest and booty, had been preparing for some time to conquer the kingdom of Serbia on their way. Under the leadership of Sinan Pasha, they led their army in front of King Stefan's court. With the new sultan and hundreds of heavily armored horsemen (spahis) and fearsome mercenaries, the army began its campaign.

The "heart" of this army were janissaries, foot soldiers who, as children, were handed over to the sultan by paying tribute in blood. Separated from their families in early childhood, they were converted to Islam and sent to study in the best schools, training daily for combat. Their loyalty was solely to the Sultan, living only for his struggle. Janissaries were fearless warriors, trained to face the toughest challenges.

In addition to the Janissaries, the army was also made up of Psetari (Shekbani), named after their original task of leading dogs for the sultan and participating in hunting. However, in battle they became the sultan's elite, guarding him as his personal guard.

Sinan Pasha, a warlike military leader eager to conquer Serbia, became the sultan's right-hand man. Wherever a serious battle was fought, his name was at the center of the action. Armored men, dressed in shiny black armor, instilled fear in their opponents from the very first encounter, while black metallic flashes from dust clouds made people flee.

The screams and howls of the startled people echoed as they spread through the air. Swords flashed like lightning and blades buzzed like thunder in a storm. King Stefan, aware of the danger that threatens his people, ordered the archers to open fire.

Hundreds of soldiers suddenly went into action, running bravely to protect their people from the Ottoman invasion. Their courage and determination were the only bulwark that stood between the innocent children and the impending doom.

The Turks advanced relentlessly towards the city. Although the peasants fought bravely to protect their homes and families, they were less equipped than the Turkish soldiers. The battle lasted only a few hours, but the strength of the Serbian army was gradually broken.

In that chaos, Sinan Pasha took advantage of the opportunity. He made his way through the enemy ranks, with the intention of personally going to the walls of the castle. With each step, his saber shook before him, cutting through everything in its path.

The horrors of the war spared neither women nor children. Sabers swung relentlessly through the ranks, and blood soon began to soak the ground. A frightened servant held Iva tightly, although she resisted, her heart longing to run home to her family. Her thoughts were filled only with the desire to return to her own, for her mother to hold her in her arms, and for her father to protect her.

The trumpets sounded, the drums beat the rhythm, but in vain. Although Stefan's army was not numerically superior, the Turkish attackers were agile and well-organized. The Serbian cavalry could not break through the densely deployed Ottoman infantry. From the walls of the castle, the brave guards threw buckets full of embers at the enemy who was trying to climb the walls.

The Turks were furious and persistent, but the Serbs also fought desperately, not wanting to surrender.

The rest of the army was trying to break through the massive wooden doors of the castle along the corrals. They pushed with all their might on the huge wall until the door gave way and collapsed under their force.

Inside the castle, courtiers and servants fled before the onslaught of the angry army. King Stephen, together with his knights and personal guard, bravely faced the oncoming force. Everything seemed like a storm accompanied by the sound of dust and metal banging as the fight took place inside the castle.

Srdan, King Stephen, and his knights, dressed in heavy armor, fought bravely. However, in the end, the force of the attackers was too great. The screams were lost in the sound of the battle and then, after a while, they died down.

The great city with its castle was forever conquered, ravaged, looted, burned and destroyed, leaving behind only ruins and ashes.

The fire was consuming him. All that remains are the fortifications of the castle that so lavishly cast a shadow over the rest of the city. In the distance, people could be heard mourning their lost city and their ruined houses.

The old servant took Princess Iva under his wing and dragged her away from danger. They quickly mounted their horses and fled as far as possible from the terrible scene that was unfolding. They ran as fast as they could, while large tears of immeasurable sadness slid down the face of the little princess, who at that moment felt indescribable pain at the loss of her family.

Without a word, Iva accepted the man who was now her only support. Through the maze of streets that rose and fell, they passed at a speed that echoed through the silence of the city. She realized that they were moving away from everything she once knew - from the castle where she grew up, from the streets she loved, from the church where she regularly went with her mother for the liturgy.

The thick sounds of galloping horses broke the silence, but the inner anguish she felt was mute, unrelenting, filled with sadness and the bitter knowledge that her life would be changed forever.

Bridges that could be crossed in the past have now fallen, and now only large pebbles of stones are left in the shallows. They ran over them with great difficulty and managed to reach the other shore. After a long hike, a new path followed. It was a forgotten road, which only the local population knew about. It was protected by rocks, over which even horses could not go. The road continued over the mountain, steep and cold, leaving the river behind, Finally they came to a mountain path, winding like a snake, so narrow that they had to go one behind the other, pulling the horse behind them. It wasn't until late afternoon that they reached the very top, where they could see the summer sun slowly descending. The moon rose higher and higher, and the wind grew louder and colder. Opening her eyes, she saw a landscape spreading before her eyes.

They traveled for two days, hiding from the Turks who were spreading across the kingdom like a plague. After a long journey, they arrived in a remote village, far from everything. He led her into a small wooden hut stuffed with straw and mud. An elderly Krsna woman, in a plain white robe, with a red ribbon tied around her waist, came up to her and helped her to bathe. She dressed her in a simple village costume and took off her beautiful royal robe, which she threw into the fire. She stared blankly at the fire as her white silk shalwars embroidered with gold thread and woven waistcoat burned with various decorations that were once sewn at court just for her.

She knew that she would never return to her golden bed, she lay curled up in the modest old dilapidated bed set up. She buried her head in the pillow and, overcome by pain and bitter tears, fell asleep.
After a few hours of sleep, they continued their journey again, running away from the Turks and hiding. The old servant led her as far as he could so that the Turks would not find her and capture her. They rode like that for a few days until they finally arrived at a place she had never heard of.

Although she was just a little girl, only eight years old, overnight she forgot about her carefree and innocent childhood. Through the stories, she learned that the janissaries had taken her brother and were training him to become their best soldier. He was sent to the Ottoman court as a tribute in blood, where Sinan Pasha took him under his wing, constantly guarding him and never leaving him for a moment.

This knowledge broke her with pain, while the queen, her mother, was in very poor health. The heavy heart of the mother and the sadness of the little princess created a darkness that enveloped the castle, while the hope of the return of the brother smoldered like a faint spark in the night. It was said that on that day King Stefan fell defending the castle until his last breath, as a true military leader and hero of the Kingdom of Serbia. His death brought a black cloud that covered Serbia forever. The time that followed was terrible for anyone who survived the massacre that day. Everything of value was taken and taken. The castle's treasuries were ravaged, food was gone, and a dark shadow of grief and despair descended upon a kingdom that was forever changed.

Farm animals were taken to feed the Ottoman army, leaving behind a once-fertile land bathed in the colorful array of vegetables and fruits that were grown. Now that land was covered in mud, ash and soaked blood. Children were abducted en masse from their homes and taken in an unknown direction towards the Ottoman Empire. Lawlessness reigned, and the fear of the invasion of the Turks was omnipresent. Rebellions were brutally suppressed, and the surviving authorities retreated to their territories. The Serbs were forced to accept the supreme authority of the Sultan and his rule.

In such an environment there was no more music or laughter, nor playful children and birds chirping. Not even the sound of playful hooves of

Serbian horsemen could be heard, nor were the epistles and ceremonies that once marked life in the kingdom taking place. Instead, there was a rather dark atmosphere, marked by loneliness and quiet anxieties about the future.

A careful upbringing and all the lessons in manners and manners had not prepared her for what was to come. Instead, the princess spent her days practicing swordsmanship, fighting and riding with the other children who were brought there, hiding them from the janissaries. Happy and carefree games have been replaced by sabers The smile on her face was long gone, and all she wanted was to see and hug her family again. Deep in the forest of that unknown little town, a vindictive plant grew. Strong and skilled as a boy, more agile than most, determined to defeat Sinan Pasha and avenge her family. Each stroke of her sword was like an expression of the deep sorrow and pain that permeated her, but also the strength and determination that drove her forward.

* * *

Years passed, and the little girl grew into a beautiful young woman. She was dressed in shalwars, a waistcoat and a gold band on her head, she wore a black uniform with gold embroidery. She rode through the forests and meadows on a black colt like a boy. A saber hung from her waist, while two swords were placed crosswise on her back. A small knife was stuck in her long arm that came out of her ankle.

No one knew who the girl was, but everyone looked at her with admiration. Only a few people knew that she was the daughter of King Stephen, and they kept her from prying eyes. Although she was forbidden to leave the village, she would deftly sneak out and make her way to the stream in the forest, as she did now.

Riding deeper into the forest one day, the sun began to hide among the treetops when Iva saw a stream. She got off her horse to water him and slowly approached the water. Then she noticed a flock of sheep bleating in the fold, looking as if they had strayed. The sheep were pure white in color, each with a bell around its neck, while fortresses spread out on the heights.

At that moment, she heard a young man and a dog barking. Soon a chubby, funny dog appeared in front of her, followed by a panting young man.

"What are you doing here?" Iva asked him sharply, almost like a sergeant. The boy smiled slightly.
"So I'm looking for my stray flock, you understand. And what are you doing here?"
"That's none of your business, pick up your sheep and move on!" Iva answered him almost offended.
But the young man with green eyes, black hair, a beautiful face and a shack on his head did not give up. "But that's impossible now! I can't gather them all by myself. Will you help me?" he asked.

Iva leaned against the horse and watched him silently. The young man was wearing white slacks, brown pants and a white shirt with rolled up sleeves. His face was kind, noble and cheerful, but at the same time it gave the impression of the strength and dignity of a warrior. He didn't look like the kind of shepherd Iva knew; something unusual was hidden in him, something that betrayed him. him the body was built like a strong young man, more reminiscent of the young knights who once attended tournaments in their city.

Iva judged that he was not much older than her, but he had something about him that made her trust him.

She hadn't done anything fun for a long time, so she agreed to collect sheep with him. They soon became good friends who regularly met at the stream, socialized, joked and looked after the sheep.

Filip's father came to Serbia and far away, he was an elderly swordsman who took his son with him. The skills he possessed and the accolades that followed him ensured a comfortable life for him. The news that a machar came to Serbia from the outside, as if she was saying that he knows how to forge differently, he makes better ones made of domestic swordsmen, spread faster than anyone expected. Everyone knew that he was the man to go to if you needed a great sword. Soon he had so much work that he even had employees. His swords were known for their extremely malleable metal, lightness and strength, from which sabers were made. Crusaders ordered them in large quantities. They were equipped with far inferior and more durable weapons that the enemy feared. The strength and beauty of the blade pattern gave them a special meaning.

His father loved his work, took pride in his swords. He tried each one individually before handing it on. Before the Ottomans burned down their house, Philip, who grew up only with his father, was trained as a real knight from an early age. He learned about swords, how to make them, and practiced with them day and night. He longed for the day to go to the tournament and prove his skill. Unfortunately, before he was given the chance, the Ottomans did not even spare his house. As much as he had strength, the swordsman defended himself, he swung and cut everything in front of him, seeing that he would be outnumbered, he decided to do the most honorable thing he could. The Turks knew very well who was standing before them, they were ordered to capture him alive so that he would do his work for them. What they didn't count on was that he would take his own life, taking the secret he was carrying with him forever. That's how Philip, just like Iva, was hidden and sent to an unknown expanse, since the janissaries were looking for him as well as Mihajla and wanted to kill him. take.

The enchanted sun slowly rose behind the glade, surreptitiously illuminating this hidden village, far from the hustle and bustle of the city, nestled among thousands of pine trees. Iva opened her eyes in a clean white cotton nightgown, surrounded by a clean bed sheet. Her broken heart was trapped inside a healthy body, like a prison with no way out. Numerous ghosts haunted her, she always woke up in a cold sweat, facing the dark day again and again - the day that changed everything. She put on a red plush dress with simple embroidery, tightened the string belt. Her braids were decorated with a red ribbon, and she lifted her riding cloak from her chair and set off alone, passing through the town. Like lightning, she sped through the narrow streets, light illuminating her path as she moved through this tiny town, cutting the streets at right angles.

Now the dilapidated and unattractive houses looked older than they really were. The once vibrant community, with playful children walking those faded streets, is now gone, as if all its wealth vanished overnight, like smoke.

All the animals they raised had to be handed over to the Turkish sandjakbegs. A portion of fruits and vegetables also had to be surrendered. All that remained were pigs for breeding, which the Turks did not want. People were forced to sell their uniforms, jewelry and family valuables that they brought as dowries. Everything that was once valuable, such as chests, furniture and large beds with wood carvings, was long ago sold and replaced with meager furniture.

It was just a carpet woven with thread, kept behind hay, hidden in deep storerooms with provisions.
She rode aimlessly until the sun was fully above her, and before her she saw ridges and slopes descending to lowlands and plains. She came out of the small valley, over the edge and down the slope beyond, reaching the bank of the winding river. She stopped and listened, at every step she could hear a flock of birds, the rustling of trees and the noise of animals.

She sat down to rest. She got off her horse and stood in front of the river. She saw her reflection in her. She was a beautiful and young girl with red cheeks, dark blue eyes like a barrel, and blond hair the color of wheat. Luxurious hair, like silk, cascaded down her back, sections gently curled into soft curls. Simple, modest ducats, without any material value, shone on her neck. The eyes, usually filled with life and light, now seemed to yearn to shed all the tears of the world. Villages is ashore, turbulent thoughts flooding her mind.

As a child, she often stared out the window of her father's castle and watched the world unfold before her. She followed the quick steps of the maids who carried the laundry to the shore for washing, and watched the grooms tenderly care for the horses. But most of all, she liked to watch Mihajlo skillfully manage the horses during training.

His skills mesmerized her as she watched carefully as he held the shield, falling from his horse again and again, bravely carrying the burden as he jumped over obstacles with ease. She watched him as he practiced his fighting skills with spear and sword. Although he was young, the prince was expected to be more skilled and prepared than many knights. He exercised more, had harder workouts and started earlier than others. He had to earn the throne one day, which would be his, there was no time to rest.

She remembered how they once allowed her to attend the beginning of a knight's tournament together with Mihajlo. While he could stay for the entire tournament, she was only allowed to see the beginning. There were many people together, more than she had ever seen before, with flags of various colors and coats of arms flying from the walls, although these symbols remained incomprehensible to her. People excitedly waited for the start of the tournament, betting and arguing with each other about who would win the title that year, both verbally and sometimes physically. Street vendors loomed in all directions, offering beer, wine and cured meats to those who had been waiting since dawn. Music came from all sides, mingling with the roar of excited horses. The horses snorted restlessly as they carried their heavy armored riders, awaiting the start with them.

As they emerged one by one, those young men were bursting with tension, their eyes bulging beneath their helmets as their muscles tensed, clutching downed spears in their hands.

Iva tried to lean forward to see each knight one by one. Among them, she recognized Mihajlo's teacher. He stood out from the others by his defiance, as the oldest among them, he was the first to approach and bow to the royal family, followed by the others. Loud cheers and applause followed their arrival. Then her mother pulled her by the sleeve and said that she had to go with the nanny back to the palace. Frowning in anger that she was too small to participate in such a big event, Iva silently lowered her head and left. With an effort she returned to the present again.

One afternoon, Iva was hanging out with Philip, riding with him through glades and meadows. Their path led them to an old wooden hut that, like an old warrior, had steadfastly resisted the test of time. But just then, rain burst from the clouds, accompanied by the rumble of thunder. They quickly dismounted and sought refuge in that cabin. Iva stood by the open window, watching how the rain, touching the ground, turned the ground into a small torrent, which gurgled down the slope.

Philip then began to tell Iva everything about his life, about the journey that led him to the moment in which he is now.

He told her unusual stories, stories that had followed him for years, while his bright eyes shone under thick eyebrows. Listening to him, Iva gradually realized that, although their lives are at first glance different, they actually have a lot in common. They both felt like strangers in the world around them, as if they had lost their previous lives.

Then Iva made a brave decision to get rid of her dark secrets and entrust him with her biggest one, the one that gripped her heart and soul. She decided to talk about everything, to tell him her story from the very beginning, who she really is and what hardships she had to go through. She found herself revealing more about herself to him, about her hopes and fears, than she ever thought she would tell anyone.

Iva's words exposed hearts and minds, often dark and filled with hatred towards the Ottomans who freely roamed the land, bringing destruction and pain - pests that kill, break, cut and burn.

* * *

After some time, Filip called Iva to meet in the forest, explaining to her that they had to talk about something important. Due to the presence of uninvited listeners, they decided to go their separate ways and meet in the clearing where they first met. The night was clear, cool and strewn with stars, while wisps of mist, like smoke, slowly slid down the slopes from the streams and low meadows. Birches with thinning branches swayed in the wind, creating a black web against the dark sky.

Philip waited for Ivo with a serious expression on his face, without his sheep. She asked him what was going on. He replied that Sinan Pasha was approaching with his army, and that he was going to join the others in the uprising against the Turks, and that she would lead the way. Iva smiled slightly and asked him who organized it, since she knew nothing about it. Philip explained to her that this event had been prepared for some time and that the people, learning that the princess was alive, decided to rise up in an uprising against the Turks, and that he was going to join them. Iva wanted to stop him and explain to him that she knew nothing about it, but he had already left. She mounted her horse and hurried back to the old servant, expecting an explanation about the uprising.

Soon she found herself in front of an old wooden door, tall and wide. She pushed open the heavy door and walked resolutely down the path towards the thatched house. People and weeping women were standing in front of the house. The old servant was very ill and called her in. Iva paused for a moment, unable to take that last step. She felt overwhelmed with emotions, like the day she lost everything, like a frightened little girl who lost everything in an instant. Fear gripped her, a witness to her curse and the hope of death. She took a deep breath, forcing herself to continue towards the bed.

It was a modest room, with a bed placed in front of the window. A single candle burned in the candlestick, casting long shadows across the wooden floor. The old servant slowly raised his head, leaning on the edge of the bed, and looked at her gently. His already gray hair fell over his face, and his white beard stood out in the soft candlelight. Gentle looks under white eyebrows watched her seriously. His stomach was shaking as he spoke to her.

He told her that at the head of the army is Sinan Pasha, her brother Mihajlo, who now leads the Turkish army. After so many years of torture, he is exhausted and no longer knows himself or his people, but blindly obeys and carries out the orders of Sinan Pasha. Sinan Pasha trusts him so much that he is no longer guarded they don't supervise. The Janissaries completely clouded his mind, they turned him against his people. Subject to strict rules and strict discipline, he was trained in the use of various weapons, including bows, sabres, spears and swords, and with constant practice, he became a Janissary, part of the elite of the Ottoman Empire. Big tears flowed down the young face of the princess, while a heavy pain passed over her lips.

"That's why you have to go, he has to see you. He doesn't know you're alive, no one does. He's the heir to the throne, our future king. You have to rescue him from the clutches of Sinan Pasha before it's too late, he has to recognize you, he has to return the crown. Only you you can save him. There is no way to save your parents, but you must at least try to save him."

The old man's soft voice full of hope spoke to Iva's soul, as it had once done to her father, nothing more was needed to be said. Iva looked down, not wanting to face him. She sat silently for a while, and then she came up and hugged him.

He was her only family now. He was everything to her. With fear in her heart for his health, she knew what she had to do.
"Come now, you need to train more than ever. Before you is the hope of the Kingdom of Serbia. Only you can save our people. Don't worry about me, I'll be fine. I feel, it's not my time yet, my time hasn't come yet. Go now, child mine, and don't worry about me."
She kissed the old hand, as she had once done to her father. She turned and started back

* * *

In a secluded cabin in a clearing of the forest, surrounded by dense undergrowth, far from prying eyes and eavesdropping, all the chiefs met, concluding the last secret meetings on the defense of the southern border and equipping the army. Among them were the most influential survivors, supporters of the king and people whose families were destroyed, eager for revenge. Their faces, battle-worn and weathered, bore witness to many struggles and trials, knowing every part of the landscape and every blade of grass in it, which would give them a strategic advantage in the battle ahead.

The response of the poor was massive. People of various occupations joined, while groups of crusaders arrived from all directions, hiding in the huts and houses of the peasants. However, of all the crusaders who arrived, only a small number were ready to engage in combat. The army was poorly equipped, almost without horses and with little real war equipment. Supply was a big problem. Nevertheless, there was great faith in this army, driven by the desire for freedom and revenge.

They discussed for a long time what should be done and how to defend against the overwhelming Ottoman force, which was far larger and better equipped. All the gathered excitement grew, almost palpably, like a current of air or a wave of heat from the desire to expel the Ottomans. The Turkish army did not wait quietly, but their scouts skilfully listened to every whisper that reached them. Preparations began almost immediately. A huge army was assembled, and the sultan asked for help from his vassals and men, as well as an adequate amount of food for each soldier. The army was led by Sinan Pasha, with the support of the most important military leaders, among whom was the estranged Prince Mihajlo.

A huge Turkish army was moving through Serbia, and the entire Serbian community was alarmed by the arrival of Turkish troops. Philip was well informed about the movements and intentions of the Sultan's army, and knowing their plans, he decided to intercept them. He and the other crusaders planned to stop the Turkish ships before they reached the coast and plunder them, thus acquiring the necessary weapons for the coming campaign. Reinforcements soon arrived, as did provisions for the soldiers.

Blacksmiths worked day and night, hidden in a small village between the slopes of the mountain, surrounded by the silence that enveloped them. They forged shields, swords, sabers, iron maces, armor and other weapons, preparing for battle. Warriors were equipped with two spears - one for throwing, the other for hand-to-hand combat, a bow and axes, while they used shields as protective weapons. They wore various armors to protect the head, neck, arms, chest, hands and legs, often decorated with headdresses in the shape of wings. The armor was formed from two plates and had a gray-black tone. Ordinary soldiers and peasants wore white linen shirts over the legs, with protective breastplates of the finest metal, and a red embroidered belt.

* * *

The morning dawned, pale, cold and damp. Life in Serbia became more and more difficult, so external action became more and more necessary.

People were tense and impatient. Iva was standing on her horse by the embankment along the road, staring into the mist to the east, beyond which lay the river. Suddenly, around the bend, a black horse came by, and on it a large man, somehow slumped in the saddle, in a large black robe with a hood. His face was in the shadows, almost hidden. When he reached Iva and aligned himself with her, the horse stopped. The rider was sitting on it quite still, head bowed, as if listening. When he realized that there was no one around who could hear them, he took off his hood and then showed himself in full light. In front of her was none other than their old groom Srdan. Iva's face suddenly broke into a big smile.

As they passed by the river bank, far from where she grew up, where she watched him lovingly groom the horses, even though he had assistants, Iva remembered how he liked to do it alone. As he said, horses understood him much better than he understood people.

His horse, always up to his shoulder, trotted after him, looking quite happy to be in the company of the groom. Since she always took care to be polite to the people in the court, she now felt that him being here with her now was almost as if he was one of her family.

"I'm so glad to see you, I thought you were dead!", said Iva with a smile. "As I am, dear child," replied the groom quietly. Then he let out a long sigh and began to tell a story that had been buried deep inside him for years, he had never told anyone. He told her about the moment they killed the king, how they fought, about her mother who was taken away. He described how he saw Prince Mihajlo in the distance, how he tried to defend his mother with all his might, attacking the horsemen.

"I died the day the king fell," began Srdan, in a voice that exuded deep sadness and bitterness. "I thought I was dead, I was lying under the bodies of fallen soldiers, I woke up, I didn't know if I was awake or in hell. But it was hell. The bodies were everywhere, the screams were silent, they were heard from all Women mourned their children, husbands, grandchildren.

The city was burning, it was burning for days. Only the fort remained of it. No one was spared. Neither old nor young. They stole everyone's life in one way or another. I don't even know how I survived. My leg was badly injured, I was wounded by a spear in the shoulder, that must have saved me, a few millimeters down and I would have been dead. At least I would join my people, my people, neither alive nor dead like this. Left to bear witness to this accursed people who crept in unnoticed. Since I found out that there is a possibility that you are alive, I have revived, since then I have been looking for you. Along the way I became ears that they listen to every noise, every whisper, every myth about you. As inconspicuous and old as this, I'm of no use to the Turks, but I am to you. I heard a battle brewing, people are whispering, I came here to make sure you're really alive. The end must come sometime. We only have a little time left.

We are surrounded by destruction and ruin, there is no escape for us, you are our last hope."

It was the hope of great danger and menace that constantly loomed over them and pursued them as they walked: the terrible threat of a lurking power, an evil lurking behind the dark veil wrapped around her throne. Iva sat for a while, trembling, as horrible scenes passed through her, each worse than the last. Her heart pounded hard in her chest, and the images began to come together one after the other: the death of her father, the capture of her mother and brother. Then she stood up, fighting with all her might not to scream, and looked into his dark eyes.

"They took everything from me, Srdana," Iva told him, her voice ringing with anger. "Everything I had. Do you understand? Everything!"
The anger in Iva's heart suddenly turned into rage, and she raised her sword in the air, shouting at the top of her voice, "I swear I will take revenge on them!!!"

* * *

Finally, that awful night fell. Everything was already ready in the city; a lot of people were shocked because the news was spread all over Serbia. Tents could be seen from the city walls in the field. The lights burned all night while people waited for dawn. And when the sun rose on a clear morning over the mountains in the east, on which there was no more hay, all the bells rang and they all rose and fluttered in the wind. Philip no longer had time or reason for that bittersweet anxiety that he had been waiting for so long. He did not sleep in a tent, but always in the open and under the sky, putting only horse blankets and samaras under his head. He saddled his horse and set off with a group of crusaders to conquer what he was most skilled at. He had long since mastered the strength of his arms and the skill of handling weapons.

The Serbian army, which consisted mainly of peasants and shepherds, consisting of ten thousand men, was opposed by 100,000 Ottoman soldiers. Each subject was equipped and had a long spear, long sword, bow and arrows and a belt knife.

Next to Philip, who was galloping with other men, horsemen rushed by, led by a black crow who was in armor. On it was a girl dressed in golden armor that covered a leather dress holding a sword tightly around her waist that was fastened. Her loose sun-colored braided hair fluttered in the wind, holding the horse's reins tightly, while in her right hand she held aloft a flag with two double-headed eagles, the symbol of the Kingdom of Serbia.

Rising above the sea of subjects and banners, she acted as an avenging angel. A battle soon ensued. The battle began in the early hours of the morning. The terrain was very suitable, on one side there were mountains with forests, and on the other side a river. One part of the Turkish army was placed on the right bank of the river, while the cavalry charged towards the Serbian soldiers. From the river came red-hot embers that fell like a fire element.

Soon the Serbian shooters also opened fire. The sky turned red, and suddenly, although it was dawn, night came. Sabers were heard, horses panting, swords striking like thunder on the field. Their detachments were found together with the detachments of the army led by Mihajlo. At that time Mihajlo was already considered a great janissary who clashed with the Ottoman military detachment under the command of Sinan Pasha. Several years in a row, he won one after another.

Two-handed swords swung above the enraged army rushing across the fields to meet the black Ottoman army. The horses scrambled and fell at the angles of the blades coming from all sides.

While the Turkish cavalry was regrouping and preparing for a new attack, new infantry arrived, reinforced. Many Turks fell to the ground impaling themselves on a sharp spear that the Serbs had placed hidden among the bushes before the battle. The strong resistance of the Serbs that followed forced the Turks to regroup. Encouraged, the Ottoman army launched a new attack, this time led by Sinan Pasha himself. Then the Serbian horsemen, hidden in the deep forest, launched an attack, attacking the Turks from the side. That part of the cavalry was led by Princess Iva. Surprised, the artillerymen turned their barrels towards the cavalry, but without success. The horses galloped, carrying their armored warriors on their backs, bowing and rearing before the Serbian flag that swayed to the beat.

The horses turned in a circle, bumping their shoulders. One rose from the sea of horses like a statue, the horse and rider charging at the other horsemen, lashing their swords in front of them. Philip noticed the princess in golden armor, which was all in gold and protected her from head to toe with a large golden shield on which was the coat of arms of the Serbian kingdom, a double-headed eagle, falling from her horse injured, holding on with her sword in her hands, trying to get up. . He ran to help her. As he approached, he saw a Turk trying to attack her. With all his weight, he crossed his sword with the blade that fluttered above Iva's head. With a strong twist and great skill, he turned his sword with the movement of his body, as if they were one, and blood flew. The Turk's head rolled across the dusty field.

He looked at Iva, who was lying on the wet grass. His face became petrified with impotent rage. He bent down and picked it up, handed it to the horse and carried it over. He got on his horse and rode away carrying the princess with him.

As he rode, he kept looking back, looking at his enemies.

The rest of the people cleared their way, striking the enemies with their swords and making a safe passage for them. They went further and further. They came to a wild path that went up the mountain. The bushes and other grass disappeared under the horse's helmet, until they reached the wide steep slopes of the fallen stones, the remnants of the landslide. As they began to descend it, sawdust and small pebbles broke off under the horses' hooves. Soon, larger chunks of broken rock came clattering down the hill, and other chunks below them.

they started to slide and roll. A great clatter of rock, churned and bounced crashing down with dust and noise. They were saved by the trees at the bottom. They flew into the shelter of a pine forest that reached the mountain slope, rising from a deep, dark valley. Soon the danger was over, the avalanche of stones ceased, and only the last muffled pops were heard as the largest dislodged stones bounced and cleared the passage deep down among the brushwood and pine roots, leaving the passage no longer passable.

* * *

The sun has long crossed the mountains. Already the shadows were deepening around them, while down in the valley, through the trees, a glowing cloud of smoke could be seen enveloping the river bank. Philip hurried as fast as he could, racing down the gentle slopes of the pine forest along a steep path that led steadily deeper into the It seemed like they were walking forever until they came upon a clearing without a single tree.

The unconscious girl began to regain consciousness. Her eyes slowly opened and she saw a shadow watching over her, she stared at it for a while until the shadow became clearer. In front of her was a rugged young man in armor with a blue velvet cloak embroidered with a golden cross, while a shield with a dragon, its tail wrapped around its own neck and a red cross on the other side, was leaning against him. She saw Philip and hugged him tightly. She was happy he was unharmed. She stood up very slowly and glanced over her shoulder for a moment. She no longer saw the enemies around her. Her head was spinning, and she was far from the battle and from knowing for sure how they got here.
"Where are we? What's going on?" She looked around, looking for her horse. "We went too far, deep into the mountain, we climbed high, the passage is impassable, it's important that you're okay. You were injured, at least I thought so, you fainted from the weight of the blow. It had to be this way."

"We have to go back," she said firmly.

She said that she was not badly hurt and that she could fight with her people. That she must save the brother she saw in the distance, that she must rescue him at any cost. Philip tore off part of the robe and bandaged the wound on her leg. He begged her to stay there safely, that he would go instead of her, but in vain, she was already on her feet ready, and the anger in her eyes was stronger than ever.

He saw that he would not be able to save her from the battle, so he firmly decided to be by her side and help her at the cost of his life.

"How are we going to get back now?" Iva wondered in disbelief, as she looked around in wonder, looking for some hidden new way. "Well, we have to somehow find a new way. If we continued like this, we would reach another foot of the mountain, from there we would have to go on foot, and it would take too long. It is a country that I do not know well. Maybe we would somehow make our way through through it and came to the bank of the river, but it would have taken us too much time, for I do not know that way, and we were left with only one horse."

In Philip's eyes, a flame flared up at the same time, his eyes sparkled. He stood up and bent his body in a deep bow. When he straightened up, Iva looked at him in disbelief, not understanding what was happening.

She had no time for jokes, time was of the essence, and they wasted too much of it. Soon it will be evening, and the chances of them coming back will be even less.

Philip brought his fingers to his lips and the whistle echoed, refracting and reverberating like an echo. The trees trembled and bent as if caught in a gust of wind. The branches bent and a huge eagle flew out of them and landed right in front of them. It was a Crusader Eagle, or Imperial Eagle whose white spots on its wings resembled a cross in flight. There have been various stories about this majestic bird for centuries. The people respected and respected her very much, they rarely saw her and she became a myth. It was believed that if you kill or injure the imperial eagle, the wrath of God will fall on those people. Although such, they were not benevolent birds.

Some were more frightening and cruel. But the old race from the northern mountains was the greatest of all birds, proud, strong and elegant. They weren't afraid of anyone, but they didn't particularly like people either.

"That's my friend," Philip told her. He approached and stroked the head of the magnificent bird, which, as terrifying as it looked, seemed completely friendly towards him. "We've been watching over each other for a long time. Come, he'll help us, he's the last of his kind, at least as far as I know. I've been watching over him for years, hiding him in these woods. I come whenever I can visit him. People don't know about him, they probably would scared them as well as you."

Come, he will lead us straight to the feet of son Pasha. Iva gave him a hand, and positioned herself behind Filip, holding tightly to his strong shoulders. And so they rose above the forest.

* * *

The afternoon also came, and the sun, leaning towards the west towards the mountain, made its way with its long yellow rays through the cracks and openings in the clouds. Suddenly they noticed that there was silence; the whole forest stood and silently listened to something. Roaring, he flew over the devastated city, leaving a shadow behind him. He was soon seen by the black armadillos as a fiery comet rushing towards them, becoming fiercer and faster. A shower of dark archers raised their bows aloft and glowing arrows began to cover the sky, bouncing off the strong quills. Then he charged straight down through the shower of arrows, ignoring them. He sneered at them like a dark shadow with outstretched wings tearing them down. He grabbed and threw horsemen with his claws.

Other birds flew from the treetops, circling and flying over the battlefield. The entire air was filled with flocks of various birds circling around. The fires around the trees shot up suddenly, rising towards the highest branches. The trees disappeared in a burst of fire. A sudden whirlwind of sparks and smoke burst forth. Soon the light from the fire became unbearable as they were high in the sky, rising in bold circles, bypassing the fire elemental that flew towards them. The eagle was forced to land, it rushed down with all its might, throwing away the Ottoman soldiers with its wings.

He landed near the bank of the river, where the flags of Turkey were flying and where the horses galloped with the shields of the army led by Sinan Pasha. The army surrounded them from all sides and began to approach with sabers, pressing them together. A shower of arrows fell on the Serbian armored personnel carriers. The bird tried to defend itself and its companions with its wings and head. Filip quickly jumped off the back and helped Iva to get off the bird. They both drew their swords and went into battle. A great cloud of dust and embers rose above them as the eagle took off.

Soon the Serbian army joined them, they broke through the Turkish cordon. The defenders threw torches at the Turkish soldiers. Fire broke out quickly and the Turkish advance was halted. Janissaries were cut off. However, it was not possible to hold back the crusaders. They came out through the ruins and broken walls of old burnt houses. The crusaders attacked the Turkish cannons, which they turned against the They immediately started looting the Turkish tents. A fierce Turkish counterattack soon followed. When the Turks entered deep into the valley, the Serbs attacked them from all sides from the nearby woods with the sound of horns, the rumble of drums and loud shouts. A terrible battle ensued, in which the Serbian armored cavalry was at the forefront. The surprised and panicked Turks could not stand it and fled towards the river and the mountain.

In front of them, like a shadow from the darkness, appeared a young man in black armor - Prince Mihajlo. Now he stood in front of Sinan Pasha, waving his saber in defense of the Serbian soldiers. There was nothing but emptiness in his eyes - they destroyed him.

He and Iva met on the street. Their swords clashed as their eyes met. Everything turned upside down - instead of standing by her, Mihajlo now stood on the opposite side of the battle. In front of her, in a Janissary uniform, stood someone whom she barely recognized. In an enemy uniform, a young man with green eyes and a large red gem fluttering above them. He wore a long black tunic, over a red waistcoat with a cloth belt on which a sword was placed, while he held a saber in his hands. The armor that covered his body made him fearsome.

He stood before her like a stranger - someone she had once loved, whom she had never regretted, and now in that uniform he seemed like an enemy to her, like the others who recoiled before her sword.

"Mihailo!" she shouted at the top of her voice, but it was too late. Sinan Pasha, who realized that the girl on the horse was Princess Iva, swung his sword and attacked Mihajlo. A chill took over her, she hardly dared to look the devil straight in the eyes. She took a step back, trying to calm the thoughts and feelings welling up inside her.

Suddenly, Sinan Pasha arrives in front of Ivo with lightning speed, preparing for another fatal blow with his saber. But Mihailo, instantly recognizing his sister in danger, bravely stands between them, preparing to confront the Turkish general.

At that crucial moment, all eyes were on the conflict unfolding before them. Every movement of Mihajlo exuded determination and courage as he strode boldly towards Sinan Pasha. His sword glistened under the sun's rays, preparing for a decisive collision with his opponent's weapon.

Every movement in battle was swift and precise, the echoing sound of metal sabers filling the surroundings as Mihajlo bravely faced the Turkish warlord. The strength and determination that radiated from Michael became more and more evident as he continued his brave fight, determined to protect his sister and his people.

At the crucial moment of the conflict, Mihailo managed to outmaneuver Sinan Pasha, boldly thrusting his sword into him. The moment of victory was filled with relief and triumph.

A great commotion pervaded the Turkish ranks after the Serbian armor bravely resisted their attacks from the rear, using maces as weapons. Although the Turks tried to overcome them, the Serbs did not give in. Perhaps they were guided by the memory of their king and the estranged Prince Mihajlo, whose presence in their hearts could not have been stronger. That memory illuminated them with a power that made them indestructible, they seemed to have reached a level of unimaginable power, which further cemented their position as invincible warriors on the battlefield.

It was this deep connection with their past that gave them the self-confidence they needed at this crucial moment. As they fought, they felt like they were part of something bigger, something that transcended the current battle. It was their secret weapon, the source of strength that sustained them at that critical moment.

After the first Turkish line was broken, the Serbian army bravely continued its advance. As they approached, a fierce hand-to-hand fight began. The ranks of the Turkish soldiers were in complete chaos, while the Serbian army was becoming more and more confident of its success.

Panic reigned in the Turkish ranks. Many tried to escape, while others were captured in the battle, surrounded by Serbian soldiers. The brave Serbs did not stop their attacks, and the Turkish army, faced with defeat, began to retreat.

The Turks tried to make their retreat go unnoticed, hoping to avoid exile. However, the speed with which the Turks retreated was not enough to completely hide them from the Serbian army. The Serbs, thanks to their courage and speed, managed to capture rich booty, including a large number of cannons, thereby significantly strengthening their positions.

Mihajlo fell to the ground with all his weight. Iva ran and knelt next to her injured brother, wiping the tears from her face. Suddenly she felt a huge bubble of remorse swell up in her chest. Philip and the others ran and placed him on a stretcher, taking him away from the battlefield to take care of him.

The eagle, the majestic symbol of freedom and strength, has returned to the forest that has always been his home. The expanse of the woods was now his refuge, a place where he could find peace and tranquility away from the blare of war horns and the clang of weapons. With its keen eyesight, the eagle watched the world spread out below it. With his wings spread in a wide arc, he felt freedom like never before.

The night was cold, Iva paced back and forth, not knowing if her brother would survive or what would happen. Her heart was pounding with fear, her palms were sweaty, and her stomach was flipping. Now the only family she had left, someone who meant so much to her, was in limbo. She was accompanied by an old servant and Philip's shaggy dog. While they waited outside, waiting for news, many other people, horses and riders stood with them. The women prayed silently and cried at the same time, listening to the prayers in agony and impatience. Hours and hours seemed to pass as the glow of the torch illuminated the darkness.

Footsteps were heard, voices were getting louder. Philip came out with a slight smile on his face. He told her that they managed to save him. "He's very weak, but he'll pull through. He asked to see you," he told her. She hugged him tightly and ran to see him.

She entered the room at the end of the corridor. Other people came out of it, women carrying bowls of water mixed with blood, and scarves wrapped around their heads. On the way, they gave her a smile, full of confidence, that she should not worry, that her worries were over. That everything will be different from now on.

She stepped hurriedly, dragging her cat across the floor. She entered the room whitewashed with long curtains that fell over the windows, letting the moonlight seep in between them. Casting a shadow towards the man lying on the bed, bandages wrapped around his shoulders and arms. She came to the bed and hugged him tightly, they cried for a long time in such an embrace. The torrents of feelings mingled again and again.

* * *

The next day, after the victory, in front of the house where they were staying, knights came carrying the confiscated Turkish flags. Mihajlo ordered them to stand on top of the fallen city walls, which would show the defeat of the Turks. Philip wanted to pursue the Turks, but Mihajlo and Srdan were against it, knowing that the few Serbs would not be able

to defeat the Turkish army in the open field, even if the Turks were retreating. Smaller groups of Serbs started chasing the Turks. What was not destroyed by the raiders was burned so that it would not fall into the hands of the enemy. Janissaries also suffered heavily.
This defeat damaged the reputation of the Turkish sultan. Once a green and peaceful landscape, it was now covered with the bodies of soldiers from both sides, with horses wandering around snorting, bearing traces of spilled blood. Both sides suffered heavy losses. The field where the battle had taken place the day before now looked like the low tide after a heavy storm.

The news of the Christian victory spread very quickly. Many hoped that the Turkish conquests had been stopped. Celebrations were ordered everywhere in honor of the victory, and Mihailo personally considered this event the most important in his life. He was reunited with his family, able to leave his previous life behind and start a new one.

The old servant sent reports of the victory, in whose glory the church bells rang in all the surrounding churches. They worked on repairing the city ramparts, supplying the city and training crusaders. These tasks were performed jointly by Mihajlo and Filip. Philip trained and equipped the crusaders, proceeding to restore his father's endowment and re-employ the remaining smiths and revive the mint again. A two-handed sword shone through Serbia again.

* * *

The sun was breaking over the glade, illuminating the kingdom with some new warm, hopeful rays. Something new, almost palpable, spread through the air - new hope. Prince Mihajlo was recovering, and with him the country and its people.

The dawn of a new day dawned, fresh, golden and promising. A white mist like autumn lay over the ground, and the air was cool. While the shadows were still long, Iva and Filip set off on their journey.

For days they rode, while the land spread around them, filled with waters that separated from the river and meandered in their beds. In the distance, with a dark peak, the mountain rose, gliding across the rivers towards the forest.

The sun was setting as they approached. There was a rumble like a thunderclap in the distance, growing louder as they approached. They reached a waterfall that in its beauty threw water over the steep rocks, flowing into a wonderful pond below. The sun's rays refracted over the jets of water, leaving the water in its blue. They were close. The road looked familiar to her.

They turned down the hill, to the path that led to the lake where the most glittering city once lay, now lying in parts scattered, burned and left to the cruel weather to surround it. It was by no means her city, which she fondly remembered, almost like a blanket in long, difficult nights, which gave her comfort and strength.

They came to a hidden place with a memorial plaque, hidden among the hills and forest. Here, under cover of night, they buried the great King Stephen in the soft earth. No one except his most loyal guards and the old groom knew about this place. Philip watched Iva place her hand on the piled earth. Memories began to flood her and faint memories of this great man. She found comfort and hope that gave her the strength to continue.

They left the grave as the sun was setting among the hills, and slowly walked away from the ruined city that disappeared in the distance. They rode on, racing the sun as it went ahead of them over hills and valleys.

Biljana Veljkovic

PRINCESS

Iva of Serbia

ISBN-978-86-906998-2-7

www.ingramcontent.com/pod-product-compliance
Lightning Source LLC
LaVergne TN
LVHW040932150826
845672LV00007B/2320

* 9 7 8 8 6 9 0 6 9 9 8 2 7 *